The Magical Bond

By Robert D. Smith and Kitty Garrity

Illustrated by Jacquie Jones

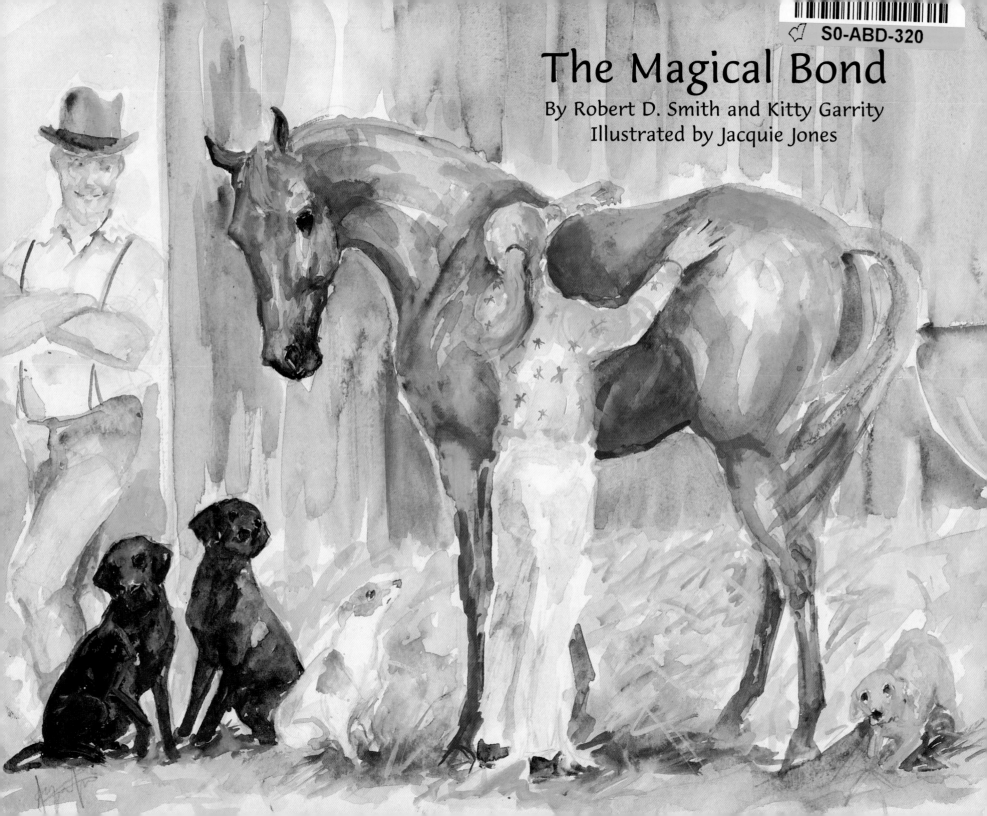

Published By
Smith-Garrity, Ltd.
P.O. Box 1273
Middleburg, Virginia 20118 USA
Phone: 1-800-800-4261   Fax: 1-540-592-3966
Email: HORSYTALES@aol.com

Library of Congress # 98-83071

Designed By:
Custom Designers, Inc.
Centreville, Virginia

ISBN # 0-9669660-0-7

Printed on recycled paper in the United States of America

To Jenna Rose, Griffin, Baby, Jeffrey, our loving families,
Jack, Guinness, India and Devon

Special thanks to Laura Rose and
The National Sporting Library, Middleburg, Virginia

Kim Berwicke loved horses, this was quite clear.
She'd helped at the stables for nearly a year.

While most girls her age were still playing with dolls,
She was grooming and cleaning, and mucking the stalls.

The work wasn't easy, but Kim did it with pride,
For when she was through, it was her time to ride.

The season was summer, in fact just mid-June.
The farm was a small one, a place called Bradoon.

As tranquil a setting should anyone seek,
It lay just south of Weymouth, near Hackamore Creek.

The owner was gentle, warm and forgiving.
No better man lived than old Mr. Cribbing.

He was blessed with a truly wonderful wife,
Who fiercely defended the local wildlife.

Farm animals included the usual troops,
Filling the pastures and paddocks and coops.

The thin, the fat, the large and the small,
She fed, cared for and cherished them all.

Morning would start the cycle in motion,
Another display of Kim's great devotion.

The girl would help with the chores till the end,
Fondly calling each creature her friend.

But her favorite of all was quite plain to see,
the beautiful chestnut mare, Gee-Gee.

Just a classic example of the mystical force,
That magical bond between woman and horse.

All great athletes share the same stuff,
Practice the basics, be mentally tough.

Learning the skills, constantly moving,
Accepting setbacks with resolve of improving.

But strong, simple faith in success is the key
To reaching, full measure, of one's destiny.

So the two spent long hours, all of that spring,
With close instruction from trainer Dee Ring.

With the hands quiet and soft on the reins,
There was flat work, and jumping, then flat work again.

Hard work and luck are both by design,
And especially so, when your teammate's equine.

After each session, Gee-Gee would merit
A pat on the neck and reward of a carrot.

But some days they would just take to the trail,
Along with good friends Martin and Gail.

Gracefully jumping historic stone fences,
While fully using all of their senses.

For Kim and the horse, with chemistry blending,
The two became one, and their star was ascending.

But with any good stew, one must stir the pot,
So it's just about time to thicken the plot.

And, in an effort to continue the rhymes,
It was rumored Ol' Cribbing had seen better times.

There surely can be no greater harm
Than the terrible tragedy — a failing farm.

In the name of progress and civilization,
We are destroying the heart and soul of our nation.

As this lack of vision continues to baffle,
We must now introduce the nasty Miss Snaffle.

Her voice sounded much like the squawk of a goose,
Most people thought she had a ring loose.

Sporting an ego too large to inflate,
Snaffle developed prime real estate.

She arrived at the farm without bringing her broom,
Cheerfully spreading the impending doom.

The aim of her visit she would freely admit,
Was turning a quick and tidy profit.

She opened the talk with the usual ooze,
"Now here's a deal you just can't refuse."

Cribbing politely nodded his head,
And listened intently to all being said.

Carrying on with more of her pitch,
"Leave it to me and I'll make you rich!"

The old man responded, slowly rolling his sleeve,
"I'd very strongly advise that you leave!"

She said, "Listen my friend, you don't understand,
Why imagine what can be done with this land?"

Spreading her arms, "I can see it all now.
Just squint your eyes and move that old cow.

"In the green valley, grand willows dancing,
Glorious sunsets and owner financing.

"Views of the mountains, a soft country breeze,
Crystal-clear streams, from the low one-forties.

"Forget half halts, leg yields and full pirouettes,
What we have here are three hundred units!"

Cribbing answered, amidst the mayhem,
"But what of the animals, what would happen to them?"

Snaffle continued, after a deep smoker's cough,
"What does it matter? Sell them all off!

"Let me remind you, you're deep in the red.
The future is now, and it's condos," she said.

"We'll finish the project by early this fall,
Complete with a convenient mini-strip mall.

"If you don't sell, the bank will foreclose,
And that will be just the start of your woes."

"Frankly, you've not long to decide.
It appears Bradoon has seen its last ride."

She continued on about who he could trust,
And then departed in a great cloud of dust.

Word rapidly spread through most of the county,
Bradoon would be stripped of her nature's bounty.

Kim heard the news while in the tack room.
Her bright shining future had now turned to gloom.

Joy and sorrow are both strong emotions,
And often encountered as we travel life's oceans.

The journey can be a smooth summer sail,
Or stormy seas, with a hurricane gale.

This foul wind would intensify still,
As more news arrived — poor Gee-Gee was ill.

She was down in her stall and hot as a pistol.
Cribbing called to his wife, "Hurry, call Dr. Bristol!"

The vet quickly arrived at the site,
And stayed with the patient through most of the night.

"It's a common condition," the good doctor started.
"I'm afraid that the mare has been broken-hearted.

"There is no medicine I can dispense
That has greater power than plain common sense.

"We must understand what Gee-Gee is feeling
Before the wound can begin to start healing.

"It's all part of nature, with this we must cope,
But without our compassion, there can be no hope."

The picturesque view from atop of the summit
Had turned dark and gray, things continued to plummet.

Snaffle resurfaced with her web spun,
Even setting the date for the public auction.

Away with the field mice and playful barn cats,
In with the workers and construction hard hats.

Our young friend Kim did her best to be strong,
But the current was swift, and the odds were so long.

Her clothes were a mess, there was straw in her hair,
She lay in the stall..sobbing..deep in despair.

But following themes we've seen in the past,
Where nice people, certainly, don't finish last.

As she clung to her dream, so it would not shatter
A husky voice boomed, "What *can* be the matter?"

Kim looked around with her eyes full of fright,
Beholding a truly magnificent sight.

A bushy mustache on a face world renowned,
That once graced the cover of _Dressage and Hound._

How could it be? Was it part of a plan?
She, in the presence of such a great man?

With a rush of emotions, the girl felt a tingle.
Could this be the one and only Sir Single?

The great horseman calmly surveyed the scene,
Then knelt as though addressing the queen.

Seeing the farm in all of its splendor,
His tone then changed to one soft and tender.

"When I had learned of Ol' Cribbing's plight,
I left for Bradoon the very same night.

"Being there for a friend, in time of need,
Is only expected of a quality breed.

"We'd met in India during the war."
This was a story not heard before.

"It was a long while ago, in time of strife,
Your Mr. Cribbing once saved my life.

"And through all these years, one lesson's been taught,
Some battles, still, are worth being fought.

"So you see, my dear, the fates had us meet,
He was a hero, and the circle's complete."

Now, instead of bulldozed, timbered and paved,
Through Sir Single's help, the farm had been saved!

Rather than acres of aluminum siding,
Bradoon became famous for Handicapped Riding.

Cribbing and wife could remain in the dell,
And Gee-Gee, of course, would live and get well.

The rider and mount once again were intact,
With posture and timing and movements exact.

And for those who believe this is only a fable,
Is that Snaffle's car pulling up to your stable?

Let's just be pleased that good will prevail,
Hence bringing a close to this horsy tale.

At the end of the day, when the course has been run,
Keep life on the bit and you'll be number one!

Glossary

BRADOON —Also spelled bridoon. A light snaffle bit with small rings used on a double bridle with a curb bit.

CRIBBING — When a horse habitually bites or chews the wood of a manger, stall or fence. Cribbing is often imitated by other horses.

DEE RING — A type of snaffle bit named for its rings, which are shaped like a capital "D."

DR. BRISTOL — A type of snaffle bit with a flat double-jointed mouthpiece.

DRESSAGE — French term meaning "to train."

FULL PIROUETTE — A turn on the haunches in the walk or the canter.
The horse's inner hind leg steps in place while the front legs form a 360 degree turn.

GEE-GEE — Child's English slang for horse.

HACKAMORE — A device used over the nose of the horse that acts by leverage. Because the hack-amore is bit-less, it is gentle on the horse.

HALF HALT— An aid used by the rider that involves a more or less simultaneous driving on using the seat and leg, and harnessing that energy in the hands by use of the bit. This will increase attention and collection.

KIMBERWICKE — Also spelled Kimbulwick. A bit that has a low port or snaffle mouthpiece, short cheek pieces and a curb chain.

LEG-YIELD — A lateral movement in two track position. The horse's body should be parallel to the long side of the arena, with shoulders leading, to assure forward movement. The horse is bent slightly away from the direction of travel. The horse's inside legs pass and cross in front of the outside legs.

LOOSE-RING SNAFFLE — A bit with larger rings than a bradoon. This bit is more movable in the horse's mouth. Available in single or double joints.

MARTINGALE— Consists of a neck strap that goes around the base of the neck and another strap that goes from the girth through the front legs through a slit in the neck strap to attach to the cavesson or noseband. The two types include running and standing, and both aid in keeping the horse's head in position.

ON THE BIT — Moving into the bit. The horse moves forward freely with a steady contact. The neck is stretched forward and flexed at the poll, increasing control of the horse.

SURCINGLE — A strap of leather or nylon used to go around the belly of a horse for lunging or vaulting. It is also used over blankets to keep them in place.

WEYMOUTH — A curb bit that is usually used with a bradoon on a double bridle. It acts by leverage in the horse's mouth.